STAR WARS™

THIS IS THE WAY

By Christopher Nicholas

Illustrated by Shane Clester

 A GOLDEN BOOK • NEW YORK

rhcbooks.com

ISBN 978-0-7364-4171-1 (trade) — ISBN 978-0-7364-4172-8 (ebook)

Printed in the United States of America

10 9 8 7

The Mandalorian was alone.

He spent his days chasing
and capturing fugitives for pay.

This was the way.

But an unexpected mission
changed all of that. He found a child!

The Mandalorian had vowed to deliver the Child to an enemy.

But his heart told him that was not the way. So the Mandalorian broke his vow and rescued the Child.

Together, the Mandalorian
and the Child blasted off on
exciting adventures.

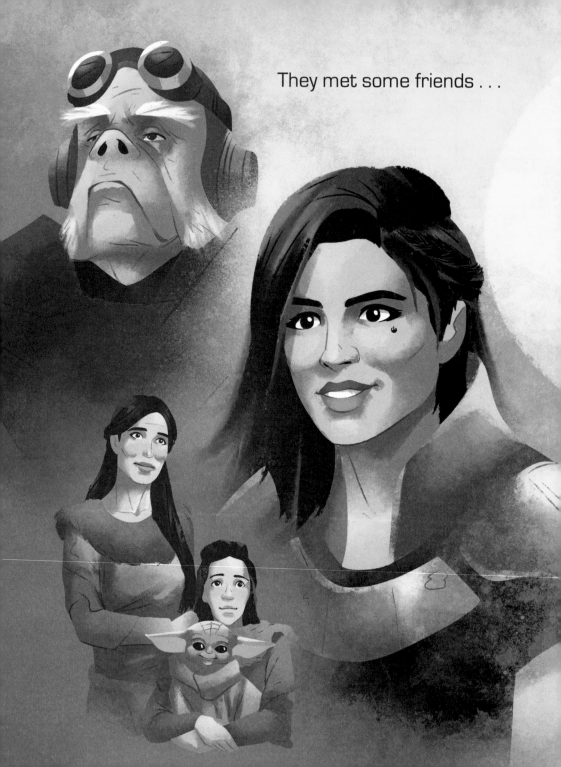

They met some friends . . .

. . . and some foes.

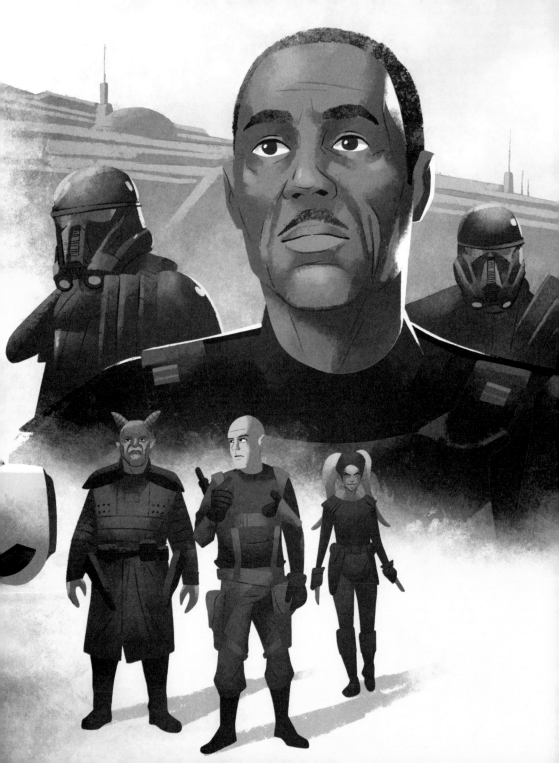

The Mandalorian did his best to
make sure the Child was happy . . .
and well-fed.

He protected the Child
wherever they went.

But sometimes, the Child protected him.

The Child had amazing powers.

The Child helped
the Mandalorian heal
his lonely heart.

And the Mandalorian
gave the Child a home.

They became a family.
This was the way.